Walt Disney's GOOFY

explores

CAVE MAN ISLAND

ABBEVILLE PRESS • PUBLISHERS • NEW YORK

ISBN 0-89659-179-4

ON CAVEMAN ISLAND

THE FOLLOWING MORNING!

BOY...THAT WAS SOME DREAM I HAD LAST NIGHT! ALMOST COULD'VE SWORN IT WAS REAL!

12-28

I CAN STILL SEE THE FUNNY LI'L GUY... SO SERIOUS ABOUT THE MARVELS HE'D DISCOVERED!

AND THEN, TOPS WAS THE AIRPLANE I'D FIND IN MY BACK YARD! THAT'S REALLY DREAMIN'!

JUST AS IF...?? ULP... WOW!!

FEELING SURE HIS EXPERIENCE THE NIGHT BEFORE WAS JUST A DREAM, MICKEY IS KNOCKED FOR A LOOP BY THE DISCOVERY OF AN AIRPLANE IN HIS BACK YARD!

WH-WHY... IT'S EXACTLY LIKE THE PROFESSOR SAID...! COULD IT BE I WASN'T DREAMING...?

12-30

...OR MAYBE I'M STILL ASLEEP ...OUCH! NO, I'M AWAKE, ALL RIGHT!

NOPE, IT'S NOT AN ILLUSION, EITHER!

AND... WELL, I'LL BE DARNED! HERE'S EVEN THE SEALED INSTRUCTIONS HE WARNED ME ABOUT!

Sealed Orders, to be opened only by Mr. Mickey Mouse, in person!

NOT ONLY DOES MICKEY FIND A PLANE IN HIS BACK YARD, BUT WITH IT ARE SEALED ORDERS, EXACTLY AS FORETOLD IN HIS UNCANNY DREAM!

12-31

SURE ENOUGH...SIGNED BY PROFESSOR DUSTIBONES! "TAKE ONE ASSISTANT WITH YOU AND PILOT THIS PLANE AS INSTRUCTED. I AM FLYING A SECOND PLANE AND WILL MEET YOU..."

and will When you gain enough altitude you must both be blindfolded.

F'GOSH SAKES! BLINDFOLDED? ???

don't be alarmed, this is a most unusual ship and will guide itself safely by radio beam. Follow all instructions to the letter. Do not delay

DELAY? DOC, OLD BOY, I'M PRACTIC'LY IN THE AIR RIGHT NOW!

MICKEY SPENDS A BUSY NIGHT, COMBING THE ISLAND FOR PROSPECTS OF FOOD! NEXT MORNING...

NOTHING WRONG WITH THIS...GRILLED TROUT `A LA PRIMEVAL!

FRIED EGG AU GIGANTICUS! 'COURSE, I **SHOULD** BE FOUR GUYS TO EAT THIS ...BUT I'M KINDA HUNGRY!

BOY...WAS I SURPRISED TO FIND THESE OVERSTUFFED STRAWBERRIES! I DIDN'T THINK THERE WAS ANY FRUIT ON THE WHOLE ISLAND!

...NO DANGER OF STARVIN', ANYWAY! NOW, A L'IL SLEEP 'TIL NIGHT, THEN I'LL GET BUSY... B-U-S-Y... BZZ-Z-Z-ZZ'N'N

PEPPED UP AGAIN BY FOOD AND SLEEP, MICKEY SALLIES FORTH AT NIGHTFALL, EAGER TO FIND A MEANS OF RESCUING HIS PALS!

HAFTA BE SURE AND LEAVE THE LATCH STRING OUT, SO I CAN GET BACK!

3-18

THE FIRST THING TO FIND OUT IS WHETHER OUR AIRPLANES HAVE BEEN RUINED BEYOND ALL RE-PAIR!

DOGGONE IT! NOT A CHANCE OF **THAT** CRATE EVER TAKIN' THE AIR AGAIN!

BUT THIS ONE'S NOT SO BAD! BY GOLLY...WITH A LITTLE WORK AND SOME PARTS OFF THE OTHER MACHINE, THIS BABY CAN FLY!

YES, SIR... JUST GIVE ME TIME AND I CAN PUT THIS CRATE IN FLYIN' CONDITION!

3-19

BUT WHAT ABOUT GAS? PROBABLY OUR WHOLE SUPPLY WAS LOST IN THE 'QUAKE!

NO, BY GOLLY! EXCEPT FOR A FEW DENTS, THESE DRUMS ARE AS GOOD AS NEW! BOY! NOW I CAN GET TO WORK!

FIRST THING IS TO STRAIGHTEN OUT THIS... GOOD NIGHT, I **CAN'T!** ONE "KLUNK" AND THERE'D BE FIVE HUNDRED CAVE-MEN ON MY NECK!